Introduction

What would you do if you were taken away from your family by dark, shadowy, hooded figures in the middle of the night; then your name erased from history, yet you still lived a life in a mystical land in the middle of nowhere? You'd be thrilled yet very petrified. So was I, but I'm a Rider one of three in the **entire** world. Riders are powerful sorcerers who can save the world from evil, only if we are united as one. Together we can over throw Apocalypse, Emperor of the darkness who brings death and despair.

Chapter 1- Kidnapped

Apocalypse has had thirteen Guardians, people who protect us, burnt at the stake (he had to use enchanted fire or else they'd survive). Apocalypse has his Dark Faces, shadowy, fast, living dead, skinny, eight foot tall creatures without mouths hunt down

Guardians because the Guardians teach us how to master our power and if we can't master our powers then we can't overthrow Apocalypse.

There's another rider. His name is Carlos. He appears about 15 years old. He is a tall, thin, pale looking boy whose hair is as black as the night with brown eyes that sometimes glow purple. He arrived yesterday; it's strange but he seems calm, like it's all happened before. If it did then why wasn't he moved here in the first place? Sometimes Carlos likes being left alone; he talks, then cries, then comes back with that strange purple glow in his eyes. Carlos seems to want to befriend me as he often showers me with gifts and shares his deepest thoughts and magic with me. As we are the only two riders staying in the Sanctuary in Daimonia, I felt we somehow should become friends, as we need to connect and become one if we are to grow stronger and overthrow the Prince of Darkness Apocalypse.

When I woke up this morning Carlos appeared a little strange, he was constantly fidgeting with his hands and appeared almost like he was walking on a bed of hot coals. His eyes flickered from purple to brown and he couldn't seem to focus on one thing. He said we needed to leave the Sanctuary now and the look in his eyes showed great fear. I wasn't sure what to do but something inside me told me to go with him as we needed each other.

Carlos is leading me into the woods. He is becoming stranger by the minute, not talking but picking up pace. There's something dark about him. I feel that the air is shifting. Something is pursuing us. I look at Carlos but he's gone! Suddenly an invisible wall hit me. I scrambled to my feet. It's a Dark Face. I'm running as fast as I can. A Dark Face is chasing me, if I look back I die because I'll probably trip over, if I keep on running I'll lose my breath and be captured. This is a terrible fate. If caught by the Dark Faces I will be burned at the stake, a slow but painful death. I have no choice but to stand and fight, but I need Carlos as together we may stand a chance. But Carlos has disappeared.

I heard one Guardian saying a few days ago that Dark Faces never lose a mission but is that true? Suddenly, out of nowhere a girl emerged out of the bushes. She had glossy, brown hair, sea blue eyes, rosy red lips and delicate but tanned skin. She looked like she was 14 years old, just like me. "Run!" I shouted. There was a yellow flash of light, and then Caleb the most oldest and trusted of the Guardian's appeared out of nowhere, like a guardian angel. He sent a message in my head saying: *get her to safety now!* But of course I didn't listen to him. He held out his left hand. The dark face let out an almighty screech before exploding into pieces of shrapnel.

Black mist appeared in front of me. Two silhouettes started walking out of the centre. One looked like a six foot man holding a boy by the hair. Slowly, the figures started to walk out of the mist, the image became clearer. It was Apocalypse! He looked like a twenty year old boy, with golden eyes and sharp teeth with metallic nails, he was holding Carlos.

"Let him go!" shouted Caleb.

"Why should I," answered Apocalypse darkly "you murdered one of my own, so I'll do the same to one of yours!"

Caleb quickly held out his staff, but suddenly the magical black mist appeared and consumed both Apocalypse and Carlos. I jumped towards it. I was able to get through the gap just before it closed. I had entered the portals time tunnel. All I could see were numbers and letters. I could hear people whispering in my ears; it gave me a terrific headache and then I collapsed!

Chapter 2 - Betrayed

When I woke up I thought was it a bad dream, but then realised I lay next to the opening in the woods. How did I get here? Caleb and the young girl had disappeared. There was no sign of Carlos or the Dark Face. I had to try and find Carlos and get us back to the Sanctuary, to warn the Guardians about the Dark Faces and how they appeared to be growing stronger.

I seemed to trek for days, unsure of what lay ahead or where I was heading. The Sanctuary seemed a distant memory. After thirteen days I finally tracked down Carlos. His decomposed body was buried under some of his and others ashes. Now without him will we ever be able to destroy Apocalypse?...

Eventually I managed to somehow find the way back to the Sanctuary, how I don't know, it was as if some dark force was showing me the way. When I walked through the gates of the Sanctuary it felt like everyone was looking at me with hopeful expressions. But just by looking at me their smiling faces soon became grim. Caleb appeared from behind the dark mist which engulfed the opening to the front gates. He clasped his hand around my shoulder and whispered,

"It's okay,"

I could feel a tear run down my cheek

"You tried your best."

I looked around me. I bet everyone in the Sanctuary was thinking: *No! We're doomed!!!*

After a week people were still either crying or blaming me for not being fast enough to save Carlos. Everyone knew one rider, no matter how strong, could not overthrow Apocalypse.

Then suddenly I felt a surge of hope rush through my body, I couldn't explain why, it was almost like the feeling you get when you see light at the end of the tunnel. Suddenly I noticed a young girl walking towards me; it was the girl I met in the forest. There was something magical and strong about her aura. Then it hit me like a bolt of lightning, she was the hope I had felt, she was the last rider!

"I guess you're the last rider eh?" I asked.

"Yes, I'm Annabelle,"

Her voice was kind of sweet and heartfelt, but I guess she was just trying to cheer me up.

"Nice to meet you Annabelle."

"You too. I'm glad you found your way out of the time portal, I thought I had lost you forever."

BANG! It came from the courtyard. Quickly Annabelle and I raced up the corridor and into Annabelle's bedroom. We looked out the window into the courtyard. Apocalypse was there but now he was different. He had white eyes, glistening skin and ripped clothes, and next to him was... Carlos! *How did he survive? How come I can see him? What the...?* All these questions ran through my head. When I looked at him closely, I noticed there was a shining black tattoo on the back of his hand. It had at the skull of a vampire just without the bottom jaws.

He saw us and smiled. We could see his murderous, canines smothered in blood. His eyes no longer glowed purple, they were purple. He had razor sharp nails and even though I was so far away from him I could smell him. He stank of rotting corpses and expired blood. What had Apocalypse done to him? Suddenly Caleb appeared looking like he was ready to take on Apocalypse alone. The fire in his eyes burned and his face had a determined look about it. I don't know what they were saying but Caleb suddenly held out his hand, Apocalypse pulled out a knife and almost like lightening cut off Caleb's hand. Lightning crackled, Apocalypse and Carlos disappeared into the black mist. Caleb's hand turned black and stony. Slowly Caleb walked back into the Sanctuary.

Chapter 3 - Despair

"What was that about?" I asked Caleb after I found him; but he just walked straight past me as if he didn't hear me.

Not only was his entire left hand black but so were all of his veins, his lips and eyes. I could just see a few tears trickle down his cheek and I knew something was wrong when he locked himself in his office and closed the blinds.

I was just about to go back when I heard a cry from his office. Now I didn't care what Caleb thought, I was going in his office anyway. I summoned my power and blasted down the door. His office was a living work of art. Old antique scrolls and posters hung on his wall. An owl clock with a living owl inside stuck on the back of his door. Hydra skin decorated the walls. Werewolf fur lay on the floor acting as a carpet. He had a huge cabinet on the wall full of trophies, delicate antiques and certificates. His desk was made of willow wood. On his desk there were priceless souvenirs and stuffed animals in a glass box which was built inside on the front of his desk. Out of the corner of my eye I spotted a metal cage holding a phoenix egg. I estimated it would hatch between two and three days.

Suddenly I spotted a dark shadow behind the desk. It was the disintegrating body of Caleb. Within a few seconds he was reduced to nothing more than ashes on the floor. I took hold of one of his pots in the cabinet and carefully scooped up what remained of him and poured it into the pot.

Right at the back of the magnificent room I spotted a burning fire. The strange thing about this fire though, was that it glowed different colours depending on my emotions. I threw the pot straight into the heat of the fire. As the pot and the ashes burnt I heard a voice in my head which sounded like Caleb's saying with grief

"I'm sorry."

I looked up thinking he was there but of course he wasn't. What had Apocalypse done? Had this great defeat made him stronger? I felt tears run down my cheeks and my eyes swell up. Other Guardians started to arrive. They looked at me with shocked faces. They thought I had finished him off. I knew what they were thinking just by looking at them. I knew what they thought - *YOU MURDERER!* Whispers started spreading among the crowd. I looked in the mirror on the wall. I saw the cruel, evil face of Apocalypse. This time he hadn't changed looks from the last time I saw him. I could hear him laughing in my head.

Chapter 4 – The Quest

Now with all the Guardians in panic I'm sure they were thinking that I must be another Phantom Rider like Carlos. I must have shown Apocalypse the way to the Sanctuary and had joined forces with him to help him become the ruler of the universe. Somehow I needed to prove to the Guardians that I was on their side, and I could be counted on to help overturn Apocalypse. The only person I thought who would believe me was Annabelle; after all she was like me, another rider. I needed to speak to her, to convince her to join me on my quest to destroy Apocalypse. Annabelle was waiting for me in her room on the west side of the Sanctuary. I entered timidly, hoping she would not blame me.

"I know it's not your fault," she reassured me. "We must join forces and become as one as it's our only hope to overthrow Apocalypse and his Dark Faces"

We set off at the weekend taking ever-lasting supplies of life and health kits. I thought if we took this quest, not only would we find out the cause of Caleb's death but also the true identity of Apocalypse.

Three days in and we were getting closer to the first clue. We heard reports from the Daily Star (which is an actual star!) that the Sanctuary had been plunged into darkness and shadows. Apocalypse was getting stronger. We had to act fast or else all of this world would be doomed.

We travelled for many days through the mountains. We travelled mainly by darkness, as it was safer. We eventually arrived at what looked like an abandoned, desolate library. It appeared out of nowhere. It rose from the ground like a great skyscraper. It was surrounded by vines and the walls were covered in what appeared to be cobwebs. I double checked and made sure it was safe to set up camp here. I thought this would be the best place to find out the history of everything. I know if I keep looking I'll find some answers soon.

Yesterday I found a secret room hidden within the library. I'm hoping it will lead me to all we need to know.

Inside it is dark, damp and dusty. When we got closer we heard talking and thought *is it really desolate and abandoned?* After we walked out from the end of the corridor the talking became louder. As soon as we entered the room the talking stopped. I knew people were here so why didn't they show themselves? A cold breeze whizzed through me and then suddenly all the lights dimmed. Four shadows were closing in on us, something was happening. All the shadows started chanting. When they came into the light I noticed they weren't of this world. They all had tattoos all over their bodies. They had no nose just slits and gills on their necks. They were truly vile and grotesque. Just as they were about to attack I remembered the night just before I was taken, stolen from my warm bed and brought to this magical land. I looked at Annabelle, she smiled and then I thought I heard her saying remember that night it will help us!

I focussed and then it became clearer. I used to believe a dragon was watching over me every night. Then when I was taken, it was there, watching me. I named it Sapphire for I thought it was a suitable name because its skin shone like a sapphire in the moonlight. The only way I could get it to come here was by calling to her in my head. I focused and whispered in my head: *Sapphire I need you, please come, PLEASE.* Suddenly there was a bang and a blast of fire. She was here.

She swooped down at the four, foul creatures who howled in pain, but that didn't stop them for long. I grabbed Sapphire and managed to haul myself and Annabelle up. She stood ten feet tall with midnight black eyes and had her shiny blue and silver silky scales. She looked like a magnificent ice sculpture. As soon as we were on her back she took off upwards towards the skylight. We closed our eyes as we smashed through the circular, glass roof. When we looked down the 'things' or whatever they were, were baring their jagged teeth and jumping up as shattered glass bounced off their wrinkly, old, yet somehow young heads. I whispered to Sapphire and we shot upwards into the midnight sky before disappearing into the clouds. Feeling air on my face was the greatest thing in the world, until I saw something that shook me to the bone and sent shivers down my spine...

Chapter 5 – The Dark Realm

The sight was terrifying to me. A burning, but never dying castle. It was Apocalypse's liar. I just knew it! He had planned this all along. He knew we would set off on this quest to find him and the answers we desperately sought. With both Annabelle and I gone, he could invade the Sanctuary and finish off the people left behind.

I could just make out two struggling figures. The two remaining Elders: Lucas and Malcolm (I really hated him). With Caleb the Supreme Elder dead they must be struggling to look after everyone. They were all gagged and had cuts and scratches. In the far distance I could see millions of dead, zombie horses which were alive, carrying crates on wheels. The people leading the horses weren't any better. In fact they were scarier. They were headless. The people in the crates were Guardians. I was expecting to see Apocalypse but he wasn't here. The castle was stranded on a tiny island floating above some lava plains. The only way in or out was by walking across a bridge made from bones. There were fourteen guards patrolling the main entrance. They were three metres tall, wore special bronze amour with spikes. Their weapons were double bladed axes, which they all carried. They looked at the Elders and reluctantly let them in with two Dark Faces. I told Sapphire to dive. We fell right down into the coldness of Apocalypses realm. Nowhere was safe now.

When we landed, Sapphire flew off to warn the rest of the population about Apocalypses army of the dead. Annabelle and I found a hollow wall. We held our breath and focused. Together we took one slow step and amazingly were able to walk through the wall. We held onto each other as tightly as we could, we knew this could be the last time we saw each other alive. On the other side it was even worse than the outside. There were cell blocks everywhere.

Crates hung in mid-air with poor, unlucky Guardians being tortured. Crows flew freely through the castle. We walked down a long, winding path with guards and cells everywhere. Together we were able to conceal our presence by using our powers to surround ourselves in a magical force field.

Eventually we came to the end of the tunnel and stumbled across the Elders who were being guarded by the same Dark Faces we had spotted walking down an underground ally. We decided to pursue them, but needed to keep our distance so that the Dark Faces did not sense our presence.

Finally they stopped at a statue of Apocalypse. The Dark Faces held out their hands. The statue crumpled into little pieces and disappeared into the ground. A secret passageway formed right in front of us. The Dark Faces pushed the Elders into the entrance and Annabelle quickly followed.

Just as I was about to enter, the gap sealed. They were all trapped!...

I searched around the area hoping to find another way in. When I was searching I thought I might've hit a trip wire or a trigger of some sort because suddenly millions and millions of Guards, Dark Faces and The Headless Ones materialised before my eyes; I was in trouble now. There's no escape.

I couldn't call Sapphire and my only companion was trapped. What would become of me now?

Suddenly the wall behind me exploded. Out of the smoke appeared three figures: Annabelle and the Elders. I stared at them in amazement.

"We're not that useless you know." Annabelle said.

All of them were armed with swords. Annabelle looked at the Elders and nodded.

The Elders dematerialised behind me, they needed to get help or we would be doomed. Annabelle threw me her sword and pulled out a long dagger from her purse which was quite impossible because her purse was the size of an orange. Annabelle and I looked at each other and charged head on at the army. When I was fighting I thought *what if this was just the patrol guards; what if there was a bigger army on the outside.*

"Arghhhh!!"

I looked to my left; Annabelle fell to the ground.

I started to run to her but I had to jump and duck as the army swiped at me with their fearsome, deadly axes. When I finally reached Annabelle her skin was pale, her lips were black and I could see her poisoned, black veins. The only way to protect Annabelle now from the slashing army was to try to create a force field around her. Luckily my powers were strong and I was able to create the field with my mind, which allowed me to continue to fight.

As soon as I killed and vaporised my ninth soldier the foul creatures I met in the library materialised in front of me with the Elders standing by their sides.

"They're here to help." explained Lucas as we destroyed more and more of the army.

"How is she?" he asked gravely.

"Her chances are very grim," I replied, "The wound is too great."

Lucas' face dropped. I could hear battle cries and explosions all around me as more and more of those foul creatures that I met in the library came. I guessed they had an entire race living here in the library. *No wonder it was abandoned and desolate* I thought. The only problem was, is that when one of the army dies and vaporises another forms in the black, sandy remains of the one who had just passed away.

It was hopeless. The power of two riders and the Elders was just not strong enough. There were only four of us left. Lucas, Annabelle, Malcolm and I. The only option we had was to materialise away from the small battle ground.

Chapter 6 – Dark Forces

The materialising felt fuzzy and I felt dizzy afterwards. When we finally materialised I found myself on the top of a peek. I started to think about the two remaining creatures. I looked at Lucas but he shook his head in grief. I found Malcolm kneeling at the side of a dying Annabelle. I wanted to see how Annabelle was coping but when I tried to reach her I felt electricity sweep though my body. I tried to keep it at bay but the closer I got, the greater the electricity got until I fell to the ground, struggling to breathe. I looked up but all I could see was a blur. I managed to make out the image and it looked like

Malcolm. He appeared to be draining the remaining life from … Annabelle!

I tried to get up but I couldn't. I started to focus, and, then, Malcolm was ripped from the grip of Annabelle's neck. He was tossed in the air then thrown back down to the ground knocking him out. What force was able to do this? Now, without his power holding me back I could see to Annabelle. When I reached her, I found two small bite marks on the side of her neck. "Lucas, help me!" I shouted.

He rushed over to my side. Malcolm stood up. While Lucas was running to me something small fell out of the pocket on his magnificent robes. When he was by my side I told him to wait there. I ran to where it fell. I picked it up and it turned out to be a voodoo doll. It wasn't Malcolm who was draining Annabelle's life it was him!

It all makes sense now. Ever since Annabelle's arrival he's been jealous because Caleb showed more attention to her than him. Malcolm held his head and moaned "Did someone throw a brick at me?"

Lucas now saw what was happening. He held out his hand and Malcolm was again tossed into the air. Huge, thick vines tripped me up and started wrapping themselves around me like a boa constrictor, just more painful. Annabelle now started sweating getting hotter and hotter as she entered the doors of death. I tried to get up but the more I tried the tighter the vines got. Malcolm got up once more and he clicked his fingers. From his fingers fire appeared. He threw the fire at me but instead of killing me the fire burnt the vines. I was free.

Malcolm and I touched hands so we could share magic. We both focused on Lucas and he was thrown into the air, fell off the edge of the peek and exploded into small pieces of shrapnel. We ran over to Annabelle, and Malcolm pulled a small bottle and let Annabelle drink from it. Almost instantly the medicine got to work. Her black veins disappeared and her skin became peach again. The sweat evaporated and she stopped shaking. *YES!!!* I screamed in my head.

Whoosh! A turquoise, marble griffin flew overhead. The beautiful, flying statue dropped a scrolled up piece of paper. When I opened it up an image appeared in the middle. It was Carlos, Apocalypse and Sapphire. Carlos and Apocalypse were whipping Sapphire cruelly with whips coated in barbed wire. It filled me up with rage. *How dare they! Those dirt blooded brutes. Why won't they die!!!* Underneath it read:

Come to the Tropical Plains and we'll do a swap; or ELSE!

Chapter 7 – The Key

We found Sapphire chained up to a spiked wall. She cried platinum tears. Her blood was bright gold. Scars decorated her body and I knew if we didn't help her soon she'd truly die. "Remember," reminded Malcolm "we go in and out no messing about okay."

We walked down a field and found Apocalypse and Carlos waiting at the gates. Carlos held the key to unlock Sapphire. "It's simple," said Apocalypse "give us the key to the chamber which protect the sceptre of eternal pain and I'll give you the key to Sapphire."

"I don't know what you're talking about." I replied.

"Yes he does." butted in Malcolm.

"Give me the key!" demanded Apocalypse

Annabelle came up behind me, she took off her necklace. It was the shape of a golden key with ruby's surrounding the handle.

"This is what they want" she answered. "The key has been in our possession for years, we were meant to keep it safe, as it has powers that will help Apocalypse rule this world!"

What was I to do? I knew I was a rider and was supposed to defend our land, but Sapphire's life was in danger, I couldn't let her die. Then I thought I heard Caleb saying give him the key, you will become stronger. How could that be?

"Give him the key Annabelle" I blurted out, "We will become stronger!"

Apocalypse let out an almighty roar. Annabelle looked at me and I smiled, "Trust me Annabelle"

Annabelle nodded and held out her hand, the golden key lying in the palm of it. Apocalypse grabbed it and again let out an almighty roar. Suddenly the chains that held Sapphire broke, she was free. As she emerged from her prison her skin healed almost instantly, we knew we needed to escape immediately. But suddenly we heard a cry from where Apocalypse was standing. In the distance I could just make out the figure of a very smoky Apocalypse. What was happening? Carlos was trying to help him, but it appeared hopeless. We decided to leave NOW.

Chapter 8 – Madman in the Mountains

When we got back to the burnt, half destroyed Sanctuary we saw thirteen Guardians rushing about. We were the only survivors of the attack. I told Sapphire to rest in the Sanctuary. It was the only safe place left for her to recover after the shock. I needed to find out what had become of Apocalypse, surely the key he had desired had not destroyed him, and there must be an answer. I had to continue on my quest, I needed to find Apocalypse and return the key to its rightful place if we were to survive.

But I needed to do this alone. Annabelle must stay and protect what was left of the Sanctuary.

When I said my goodbye's I materialised. During the materialisation I felt a stabbing pain in my stomach. I thought it happened when everyone materialises. When I arrived I noticed I had a nose bleed and when I looked down into a puddle I saw a reflection of Apocalypse and Carlos smiling down at me. But when I turned around no one was there but I swore I saw something. I got up, relieved the pain had stopped. I began walking down the crumbling road. Every step I took the road behind me just vanished.

"No turning back then." I said to myself.

Along the way another messenger griffin swooped over my head. This time it was red. Again it dropped a scroll. When I opened it, it read:

Please help rider. I need your help.

On it a picture showed where he was. I looked up and saw it wasn't far from here. But I was wrong it was an optical illusion.

The walk was long and dusty; the climb seemed to go on forever. I was sure the person who sent me this lived deep inside the heart of a mountain. Whenever I reached the opening to the heart of the mountain it seemed to disappear. The climb seemed impossible.

Finally I had reached my destination. The 'house' was like a huge dustbin. Clothes were scattered across the room. There were smashed cups and plates lying around. It looked like a living hell. In the corner there was an old, frail man. He was bent forwards over a long stick which was two times taller than him. He was about eighty years old, four foot tall and didn't have a face. Just a blank canvas with a mouth.

"You said..." I told him just before he interrupted.

"I need you" he replied.

"For what?"

"To tell."

"To tell what?"

"Secrets."

"Like what?"

"I need you."

"Yes, I know."

"Secrets"

"What?"

"I need you."

"I KNOW!!!" I shouted. "Did Georgie Worgie do wrong?" Georgie Worgie asked.

I just sighed. I couldn't just sit here. Could I?

"Listen," I said firmly "Apocalypse is strong. Half of this island is dying. Either you help me or I'll, I'll, I'll..." I couldn't think of anything else.

Georgie Worgie looked at me ashamed of himself. Suddenly slits formed where his eyes should be and they glowed red.

"Apocalypse is here. He's inside you. He's killing you slowly. You must leave. While you're here his imposter is planning war."

"What imposter?"

"Apocalypse is trapped inside you. He's using *you*. Caleb died for *you*. It's all about *you*." Slowly his body started to catch fire. BANG.

Georgie Worgie burst into flames. I looked at his ashes on the floor. When I looked up I was amazed to find Carlos standing there staring at me. How could this be? How could Carlos know where I was?

Carlos began to speak.

"You are clever; you think you have discovered the truth."

What was he talking about, what truth? Carlos continued.

"I had to kill Jason Foster the imposter. Then George Wood, the old man. Now I will kill you Leo Lewis."

Was that my name? Leo Lewis? My own name and I didn't even know it. There had been a huge piece missing from inside me, till now. Now I knew all I needed to know. I was full again.

Carlos held out his hand and a never ending swirl of black smoke shot out of it. I crouched and threw my hands over my face and head. I looked up and I saw all of the smoke revolving around me before disappearing behind me. Before long the never ending supply of shadows stopped. I now knew we were doing a traditional (but now banned) wizards duel. As soon as we start we can't stop until one of the wizards die. It was my turn. I saw a fire place with a burning fire and coals. I threw out my hand and one of the coals flew towards me. I caught it. Then I closed my hand. I told Carlos "I'm sorry about this."

Carlos couldn't make a force field, his powers were weak. The hand with the coal in faced Carlos. When I opened my hand an explosion of green fire blasted out. Like Carlos' it didn't stop. I heard screaming from inside the fire. Finally I stopped but when I did, when I saw Carlos, all of his injures were healing. I looked in fright as Carlos approached. He pulled a poisoned dagger from his sleeve. He threw it at me. It flew towards me dangerously. Luckily I caught it and threw it back to Carlos.

Carlos was an idiot. He was dumb even though he thinks he can do everything ten times better. So being an idiot he tried to catch it but it slipped from his grasp and plummeted towards his chest. He screeched an ear piercing scream as his body started to become no more than dust. As his body stated to vaporize his eyes turned back to normal while he kept on screaming, "*Malcolm, Malcolm, Malcolm is, he is the, the last rider. I, I was, I was possessed by a, a child of the flame. To infil, to infil, infiltrate the Sanctuary*". Then he disappeared.

Chapter 9 – Darkness Within

I looked out of the window at the mountain. Slowly the sky started to turn dark and grey. Mist surrounded the room rising at every second. In my head I heard the faint voice of Carlos. *My death has ignited a war. Only one can survive. The others shall enter 'THE DOORS OF DEATH...'* Then he laughed before the room was silent. All alone it was quite eerie as the mist thickened and rose. Lightning crackled in the sky. The lightning was blood red. Every strike it made hit the mountain like it was trying to get in. Smash! The window shattered into a thousand pieces. There hovering just outside it was Sapphire.

Now, even though the sky was dark she still glistened like a thousand diamonds in a cave. The lightning was getting closer with every second. I held out my hand and felt the air moving underneath me. I looked underneath me and saw I was flying! Knowing this I launched myself towards Sapphire. Her catching skills were a lot better.

I held out my hands and let the air run through my hair as we soared into the gloomy sky. Even though it was dull, my body was full of energy.

"Aarghhhh!" I screamed as the lightning struck me.

I slipped off Sapphire. As I fell a dark shadowy figure fell out of my head but when I looked at it, it vanished into the darkness underneath me. I was falling further down, down, down into the shadows below.

Sapphire swooped down and caught me. We flew over some volcanic plains until we reached the battle field. The battle field was like a huge, supersize chess board. It was made up of two colours, red and black. Below us fires raged, people disappeared and portals to the underworld opened. Sapphire let out a blood piercing cry as we were struck by five bolts of lightning at the same time before we started to fall further and further…

CRASH!!! Sapphire and I landed with a bump. I was trapped by Sapphire's body from my chest and below. Sapphire lay lifelessly, but I knew she was alive as I could hear her faint cry. In the distance a dark, shifting, shadowy figure walked towards me from out of the mist. When he got closer he looked just like… me!

His voice sounded like mine just darker, blood thirsty and ruthless. I knew this when he said "I'm your past, present and future.

I'm your fear and hate. I'm your darkness within. I'm APOCALPSE!!!"

"Where'd you come from?" I asked.

"You, I'm you, but better." he answered.

I started to wriggle. But, the more I tried the more tired I got. "Enough!" he shouted.

It all made sense now. The key Apocalypse desired was not just power to him; it was the key to my heart. If he unlocked it he would be able to control me and my powers and become more powerful than ever. I could not let this happen; the world was depending on me. If only Annabelle was here! What could I do? I felt too weak to fight, there was no escape now!

A red flash flew from his body and entered mine. I froze for a moment. Knowing how dangerous he was. He dipped his hand in a puddle. The water changed into a black sword. He held it above him ready to strike. I closed my eyes...

Acknowledgements

I would like to thank my family for their support whilst writing my first story.

The Riders – Darkness Within

Written by Jordan Gill Age 11 (2011)

www.ingramcontent.com/pod-product-compliance
Lightning Source LLC
Chambersburg PA
CBHW071224130626